Demonic Contract
Dragon Kissed Trilogy, Book One

CATHERINE BANKS

Demonic Contract
By Catherine Banks

Turbo Kitten Industries™
P.O. Box 5012
Galt, CA 95632
www.turbokitten.us

Catherine Banks
www.catherinebanks.com

ISBN-13: 978-1-946301-10-9

ADULT

Demonic Contract

The Last Werewolf

Dragon's Blood

Centaur's Prize

Ciara Steele Novella Series
True Faces
Barbaric Tendencies

YOUNG ADULT

Artemis Lupine Series
Song of the Moon
Kiss of a Star
Healed by Fire
Taming Darkness
Artemis Lupine The Complete Series

Little Death Bringer Series
Mercenary
Protector

Pirate Princess Series
Pirate Princess
Princess Triumvirate

Daughter of Lions

Lady Serra and the Draconian

DEDICATION

To my readers, new and old: Thank you for taking a chance
with a new author. I hope you enjoy my stories.

CHAPTER ONE

"This one better not be a troll like last time," I threatened my best friend Emily as we headed to a double date with yet another of her boyfriend's friends as my blind date.

"Hey, Tim was a very nice troll," she countered.

"Yes, but you should have remembered that trolls and my kind don't get along," I said and whispered the last part. No one knew my full genetics except for Emily and hopefully that was how it would stay for the rest of our lives.

"I thought that was just a family feud type of thing and that you would be fine."

"I'm not racist," I growled at her. "Our kinds can't be around each other without getting into a fight."

"I noticed when you punched him in the face and broke his nose halfway through dinner," she said with a glare at me.

"I waited as long as I could. It hurt." So, had his face. That was the ugliest man I'd been forced on a date with yet. "He was being rude to me as well, if you recall."

"Well, I promise this one will be much better. In fact, I'm really excited to see the two of you together."

Emily was a matchmaker and had been since elementary school. Most of her matches were actually very

1

successful and long lasting, but it seemed that I was a bit of a problem for her.

"Are you going to give me any info on this guy? You won't even tell me his name or anything," I grumbled at her.

She looked over at me, eyes roving from my black strappy heels to my tight jeans and then to my red, silk blouse with a bit of cleavage showing. "He's going to love you in that outfit," she said and gave me a devilish smirk.

"I bet he'd love me more out of it," I said.

We stared at each other a moment in silence and then burst into a fit of laughter.

"I'm glad to see you're both in such high spirits tonight," Dave said from where he was leaning against a pole outside the restaurant.

"He's not a troll, right?" I asked him.

A smile spread across his face and he said, "Trust me, you're going to love him."

"After seven terrible blind dates with you two, I've lost all my trust," I said. It was a lie, even if the dates they paired me with were completely not my type, I loved spending time with Emily and Dave.

Dave walked up to Emily and kissed her cheek. "You look more beautiful every time that I see you," he whispered.

They were nauseatingly cute and I enjoyed their always positive and happy relationship.

"I like this shirt," she told him and made a purring sound.

"Hey, I'm still here," I reminded them.

"Where's your friend?" Emily asked Dave.

"Really? You're not even going to tell me his name before he gets here?" I asked them.

"He's almost here," Dave said.

"Come on, Dave. Spill!" I begged him.

"He's not a troll," he replied and then laughed at my scowl. "Tora, relax. I swear this one is perfect."

"I'll be the judge of that," I grumbled and adjusted my shirt.

"Maybe we should get a table so it's ready when he arrives," Emily suggested.

"Sounds good to me. I'll come inside with you," I offered.

We left Dave outside to wait for his friend and went into the busy restaurant. Emily put our names down and smiled at me. "You don't need to be nervous. You're amazing and he is going to be blown away by you," she assured me.

"Please tell me he isn't a vampire," I begged.

"No, I promise that he isn't a troll or a vampire," she said and then bumped her hip into mine. "He's here."

I turned around to face the entrance and my nervousness ramped up even more. The man walking in next to Dave was tall, six foot two at least, muscular enough that he had to work out several times a week, had black hair and sparkling green eyes the color of shamrocks. His aura was intense and he looked like power was coiled within him, waiting to be let free to devour its unsuspecting victim.

"I love you," I whispered to Emily before they were close enough to hear us.

She giggled and then Dave stepped forward to stand between his friend and I. "Tora, this is Edan. Edan, this is Emily's best friend, Tora."

Edan extended his hand and I reached forward, expecting to shake hands, but instead he pulled my hand up to kiss the back of it. "It is a pleasure to meet you. Dave has talked about you many times, but never did he mention how beautiful you are."

"Thank you," I replied. This guy was smooth. He was also shielding his powers and keeping everything contained so that nothing touched me, which was incredibly considerate.

"Shall we?" Dave asked and motioned at the hostess who had come up behind me at some point during my meeting of Edan.

"Well, it seems that I am at a disadvantage," I told Edan.

"How so?" he asked and pulled out my chair for me.

"You have heard about me, but I didn't even know your name until you arrived."

Edan glanced at Dave who was studying the menu like we might be quizzed on it by the waiter. "Really?" he asked.

"Also, I have no idea what lies or embellishments Dave told you. For all I know, he could have lied to you," I said. I decided on a steak for dinner and set my menu down.

"I wouldn't lie about you," Dave said. "And I have nothing bad to say about you."

I tilted my head to the side and looked at him.

He laughed and said, "I swear I never mentioned those stories."

"Those stories?" Edan asked.

"Drunken stupidity," Emily offered.

"Thankfully since you didn't know my name, that means he hasn't told you any of my embarrassing stories either," Edan said with a smile.

He was hot. Scorching hot.

The waiter came to take our orders, but as soon as he saw Edan, he started shaking slightly and then bowed to him before walking away. I looked at Emily and Dave to see if they noticed the strange interaction, but they were talking casually. Edan didn't seem to notice either. Who was this guy?

"So, where are you from?" Edan asked me.

Hell. "I lived with my dad until I was about twelve and then moved up here with my mom," I answered vaguely.

"Are you in college?" he asked.

"Yes, I go to college with Dave and Emily," I answered.

He looked incredibly shocked. "You go to college with us?"

Us? "Um, yeah. I didn't know you went to college with us too." How could I have not seen him before?

"I find it very hard to believe that a creature as beautiful as you, was walking around the college and I never saw you," he told me.

I looked over at Emily and asked, "How has he never been brought up in our discussions?"

She fidgeted nervously and I sent a tiny lightning current into her thigh. "Ouch," she growled. "We had to make sure that you had actually severed ties with *him* before we introduced you to Edan."

"You kept us apart," Edan whispered in disbelief.

"We had a good reason," Dave said defensively.

"I was trying to protect you," Emily said urgently.

I raised my hand and they all relaxed. "Thank you."

Edan looked at me in disbelief. "You're thanking them?"

I looked around the restaurant and saw quite a few tables openly watching us and listening. "Could I talk to you for a moment outside?" I asked him.

He nodded and followed me out into the cool night air. Once we were away from most of the people milling about, I turned and face him fully. "They were protecting us both," I explained.

"How so?" he asked. "How was purposefully keeping us from meeting a protection?"

"Last month I ended a contract with a demon lord. I never let them know the exact specifics, but I fulfilled my obligations so the contract ended. They didn't know that part, but they were keeping us apart until they were sure that I was really free of him and the contract was really voided."

"Who was your contract with?" he asked.

"That's personal," I whispered.

"Is there any way that he could reestablish the contract?"

I shook my head. "All of my ties to him are completely severed."

"What were the conditions of your contract?"

"Edan, I hardly know you…"

"I should be allowed to know what I'm getting into," he said and then softened his tone. "Please."

"I was his assassin," I whispered.

Edan's eyes widened and he asked, "Was that all?"

"Yes," I said and then understood what he was asking. "Oh, no! It wasn't that type of contract! I was his assassin and that's it. There were no…*relations*."

He laughed and said, "I'm sorry. I just had to know."

I exhaled loudly and said, "Geez, I'm not that type of girl."

"No, just an assassin," he replied with a smirk.

"Does that bother you?"

He shook his head and walked closer to me. Slowly, he picked up a piece of my hair and lifted it so that he could smell it. "No, it makes you much more interesting."

"Who are you?" I whispered as chills swept up my spine in a warning of this man's danger.

"That is something that I hope for you to learn over dinner, tomorrow?"

He was asking me out on another date when this one had barely started?

"What time?"

"Six."

His scent was heady and manly. If I could bottle that scent, I would have bathed in it.

"We should head back inside," he whispered and took a step closer to me.

I wanted to kiss him and see if his lips were as soft as they looked. His control slipped and a bit of his power washed over me, making me gasp in surprise and excitement. So. Much. Power.

"I'm sorry," he whispered and started to step back from me.

I stepped closer to him and whispered, "How much power do you have?"

"Enough," he answered in a promise.

I let my shield slip a bit, my power coursed through me and then I let him sense it.

His eyes widened and then glowed from his power. "Who are you?" he asked, mimicking the question I had asked him a minute ago.

"You'll have to find out," I whispered huskily and then stepped around him and into the restaurant. The people who had been snooping on us earlier were all looking at me again when I came back. I hated gawkers. I didn't know who Edan really was, but they had no right to invade our evening like this. With a flick of my fingertip I sent lightning into each of them and watched with satisfaction as all of them looked away.

Edan entered the restaurant and everyone kept their gazes averted. He looked around suspiciously a moment and I smiled innocently at him before taking my seat.

"So?" Emily asked.

"We're good," I assured her.

The rest of the meal went by uneventfully right up until the check arrived. I tried to pay, but Edan refused. We went outside and were met with a group of girls who surrounded Edan as soon as they saw him.

"Excuse me a moment," he requested of them. He walked over to me, bowed over my hand and kissed it. "I had a wonderful evening with you tonight and I look forward to seeing you tomorrow evening."

"Thank you for dinner." I wanted to tell him there was no way I would go out with him now that he was ditching me for these skunks, but surprisingly he didn't go back to them. Instead, a black car with fully tinted windows pulled up to the curb and he climbed in with one last look at me and a smile.

"Who is she?" one of the girls asked.

"Are they dating?"

"No! He hasn't dated anyone since he moved here!"

Emily grabbed my arm and pulled me away from the herd before I could ask them questions about Edan. "That seemed to be a success."

"I cannot believe you were able to keep me from seeing him," I told her a bit proudly.

"It wasn't easy," Dave admitted from Emily's other side.

"Well, I appreciate the gesture. You should know that my contract was fulfilled and that was how I severed my ties with him. There's no way I'll ever be involved with him again."

Emily gasped. "Really?"

"Yep."

"Well that would have been good to know," Dave muttered.

Emily said goodbye to Dave and we went to our dorm room to change and relax.

"What did you think of Edan?" she asked me as we shared a bowl of ice cream.

"He's gorgeous and powerful," I replied.

"Dave said he doesn't even know how powerful he is, that he only experienced a fraction of his power and it was terrifying."

"I felt a fraction of it today and it was unbelievable."

"That's what got you all worked up?" she said with a laugh.

"You have no idea," I muttered and ate another big spoonful.

"I don't understand you people enjoying being around someone powerful like that. It creeps me out," she said and shook her body.

"It's knowing that they're dangerous. Knowing that he could do some serious damage to you or anyone that tried to mess with you," I explained.

"Weird."

"He asked me out on another date," I told her.

"When!" she screamed.

"When we went outside and talked about the contract."

"I told you he'd like your outfit."

We laughed and then we turned on trashy TV shows until we both fell asleep on the couch.

CHAPTER TWO

"Get up!" Emily screamed at me.

I leapt up and was ready to fight in an instant.

"What's going on?" I asked as I looked around the empty room.

"It's five o'clock," she yelled from our room where I could hear her rummaging through my clothes.

"What?" I asked groggily. I looked over at the grandfather clock she had brought from her home and then ran to the window. "Five at night?" I screamed.

"Yes!"

"How did I sleep so long?" I asked her.

"You looked really tired when I left to meet Dave for lunch so I let you sleep. I didn't know you would still be sleeping or I would have woken you before I left."

I yelled angrily and rushed to shower and get ready for my date. I had been tired a lot recently, but I couldn't remember the last time that I'd slept for so long.

The shower helped clear what was left of my sleep fog and I was slipping on my shoes when our doorbell rang.

"Critique?" I asked Emily and spun in a circle in front of her.

"Behave," she ordered and then shoved me towards the

door.

I growled at her and straightened my shirt before opening it. Edan had looked good yesterday, but today he looked even better.

He gave me a once over and smiled wide. "Are you ready?"

"Yes."

"Bye! Have a good time!" Emily called as I shut the door.

"So, where are we going?" I asked him and tried to sneak past his defenses to see his magic. His barrier was strong and reinforced.

He tilted his head to look down at me and said, "If you don't stop trying to break my shields, our date will have to continue in a more isolated location."

"I don't know what you're talking about," I lied and walked confidently with my eyes focused in front of me.

"Of course not," he whispered. The ghost of a hand slid across my lower back and it took all of my control not to turn to look at him. I knew he hadn't touched me with his hand and was using his magic. It made me wish this wasn't our second date.

He led me to the car I'd seen yesterday and a man in a black suit opened the door for us. We climbed in and I stared at the expensive leather seats, privacy window, and champagne.

"Do you have a preference for dinner?" he asked me.

"No, I like everything."

He tapped the window three times and the driver took off.

"Should I be sitting here?" I asked and lifted myself up slightly off the seat.

"What?" he asked.

"I'm just wondering how many women have gotten into this car and thrown themselves at you immediately afterwards," I said with a teasing smile.

He laughed, pulled me down, and said, "I have a very good detail company."

"You would have to," I muttered.

"Tora, why don't you start by telling me about yourself," he suggested.

"What do you want to know?" I asked. I turned so that my back was to the door so I could see him better.

"What are you studying at school?"

"I don't have a major," I admitted.

"What?" he asked, perplexed.

"I'm just going to college for fun and for some general education."

"What are your plans for the future?" he asked. "Don't you have a specific job planned that the education could assist with?"

I looked away from him a moment and then whispered, "I have plenty of experience in my line of work already."

"You don't have to be an assassin," he said, but he was the first to say it without judgment in his tone. "You could do anything you put your mind to."

I had something on my mind that I definitely wanted to do.

"I appreciate that," I whispered, "but I have little say in this."

He tensed. "I thought you said that your contract was finished?"

"It is," I said quickly, "but my father has plans for my future."

"Who is your father?" he asked.

I couldn't answer that.

"What are you majoring in?" I asked without answering him.

"Business. I will be taking over the family business when my father passes," he answered.

"What year are you?"

"Third. You?"

"Same."

He laughed a second and asked, "How did they manage to keep us apart for three years?"

"Emily can do anything when she's determined." I paused and asked him, "Have they taken you on other blind dates with horrid people?"

He thought about it and said, "Now that you mention it,

yes."

"They're good," I whispered and laughed hysterically.

"Care to explain?"

"Emily has had it planned for us to date from the beginning. She's been making us go on horrid blind dates until we finally met."

He smiled and picked up a piece of my hair, twirling it around his finger. "I think it was a good plan."

The car stopped and we walked into Ernesto's, the fanciest restaurant in town. As soon as we were away from the car another man rushed forward and bowed to Edan. "Your table is this way, sir."

I looked at Edan, but he just smiled, set his hand on my lower back, and gently ushered me forward. A bit of my power escaped, zipping up and into his hand, but he didn't remove his hand or say anything. The host led us past the full restaurant where I received many glares from women and stares from everyone. We went back into a private room which had a single table with candles and a red rose on my plate, and a beautiful view of the Lake Tahoe. Despite all of the changes that had happened, the lake remained the same, pristine blue.

"What refreshments can I get for you?" the host asked nervously.

"Water with lemon," I ordered, pulling my attention away from the lake.

"My usual," Edan ordered.

He pulled out my chair for me and then took his seat across from mine. I picked up the rose and smelled it, it smelled like him.

"I'm sorry for zapping you," I whispered as we looked over the menu, "that was unintentional."

"I barely felt it," he said with a smile that could have turned me into a puddle of goo in my chair.

The host brought our drinks and then the waiter came in. This one wasn't shaking and seemed to know Edan. "Good evening, sir and miss. Have you made a decision?"

Edan handed his menu to the waiter and asked me, "Are

you ready?"

I nodded. "I'll have two chicken tacos with refried beans."

"The usual for you, sir?" he asked Edan.

"Yes."

The waiter left and I met Edan's gaze across the table. "You sure do know how to impress a girl."

He smirked and asked, "Why do you assume that I have been dating many women?"

I waved my hand to encompass all of him. "Because, you."

"I'll take that as a compliment," he said and his smirk turned into a smile.

"It was."

"Well, for your information you're the first girl that I've taken on a date aside from the ones that Dave and Emily forced me to attend."

I didn't respond and instead leaned back to put my napkin in my lap. If he wanted to lie to try to make himself appear better, he was talking to the wrong girl.

"Don't believe me?" he asked.

"I find it poor manners to call a man a liar when I have no proof against his claim," I stated simply.

"You really don't know who I am, do you?" he asked softly and looked at me with a mystified expression.

"Should I?" I asked curiously. He was obviously rich and his family must be influential, but that wasn't very specific.

"Well, everyone knows my family," he stated simply, not bragging, just a statement.

"Sorry, there are a lot of elite families and clans," I said and shrugged. "It's nothing personal."

Our food was delivered and we ate in relative silence.

"Dessert?" the waiter asked.

"Cheesecake," Edan ordered.

I loved cheesecake.

"So, when you aren't being hounded by fan girls and gawked at by strangers, what do you do?" I asked him.

He laughed softly and said, "I spend time reading or exercising. I've been working on my martial arts skills lately."

Interesting. "Is that how you met Dave?" Dave was an excellent martial artist, especially for a human.

"Yes, actually. He was the first to hold his own against me."

Bragging.

"Maybe we could spar one day," I suggested. "I'm afraid that I might be getting rusty."

"Dave warned me about you," he said smugly and folded his arms across his chest.

"What?"

"He told me not to let you convince me to spar because once we did, I would want to marry you on the spot."

I had been taking a drink of my water, but it went down the wrong pipe and caused me to choke and sputter. I wiped my mouth with the napkin and said, "Dave likes to embellish his stories."

"I don't know, I think he might be on to something. If you're as powerful as I think, and as skilled as Dave says, you may be just the kind of girl I've been looking for."

"A bit presumptuous, don't you think?" I asked with a smirk. "I could be a psychopath."

"Aren't we all a little bit?" he asked and smirked back.

The door to the room we were in was flung open and a red goblin barged in with a snarl on his face. He had a sword on his right hip and a whip on the left. He stormed towards Edan who looked at him with a bored expression.

"You son of a bitch!" the goblin yelled.

Edan asked, "What is your issue, goblin?"

The goblin turned and looked at me with a scowl. "On a date, huh? Sorry, hun, but your date is over. Beat it."

"I haven't had my dessert yet," I told him calmly.

"Excuse me?" he growled.

"Would you like me to take this outside?" Edan asked me.

"No," I said honestly.

Edan bowed his head to me and stood up to face the goblin. "You've interrupted my date and that's very troublesome for me. You see, we were having a great time and I was finally getting to know this lovely lady, but you've ruined the mood."

"I don't give a shit about…" the goblin began, but I interrupted him.

"If you make this fast, we might still have time for a walk," I tempted Edan.

His eyes flared and in the next instant the goblin was pinned to the floor while Edan kept eye contact with me. "Your wish is my command."

"Screw you both!" the goblin yelled and hit the button on a small cylinder he had in his hand.

Edan reached for it, but the gas had already begun to spread from the cylinder and as soon as the gas touched my skin I felt like I was being boiled. I refused to scream despite the feeling and dumped my glass of water on my arm and leg that the gas had touched and then ran to the other side of the room.

The goblin was dead when I looked back and the canister and Edan were gone. I looked down at my flesh and hissed, it looked as though I had been burned and smelled terrible.

"We should take you to a healer," Edan said and I leapt back from him. I hadn't heard him or seen him enter. "Easy," he whispered.

"I don't need a healer," I told him and raised my arm so that he could see my body repairing itself. I looked at his puckered flesh on his face, rested my fingertips against his cheek, and asked, "Do you need one?"

He smiled and kissed my fingertips. "A few minutes and I'll be perfect again."

"That's some ego you have there," I teased him to try to hide my arousal. He had barely touched me and my body responded to him.

His skin healed fully the next moment and he was perfect again. "I am in your debt," he whispered and ran a hand up my formerly injured arm. "I delayed his punishment in an effort to impress you, but only ended up getting you hurt."

I raised my arm and said, "I don't see any injury."

"One boon," he whispered. "That will be my payment."

His scent was surrounding me and I breathed it in deeply, filling my lungs with it. He moved closer to me and slipped an arm around my waist. "One boon?" He nodded. "Tell me who you are."

He tensed and then chuckled softly. "May this wait until we begin our walk? Our dessert is here."

I pulled away from him quickly and returned to my seat to see a cheesecake with chocolate and caramel drizzled over the top. "I love cheesecake."

He joined me to eat our dessert. When we finished, he led the way out of the restaurant. "I don't have a jacket," I whispered as the cold night air hit me.

"Not a problem," he whispered.

I looked at him in question, but he just linked our arms and led the way away from the restaurant, down the street, and to the park that ran along the lake, which was empty at this time of night. We walked deeper into the park, away from passersby, and he stopped. He released my arm, took a deep breath, and then heat began to permeate from him. When he opened his eyes, they were glowing brighter than I had ever seen them. The heat from his body chased away the night chill and warmed me instantly.

"That's a handy trick," I whispered in shock.

Was he a demon? A fire mage?

He held out his hand and I gladly put mine in it. We walked down to the lake in the dark and all of the creatures hid from our view. I didn't know what he was, but as we walked, I knew for certain that we were the most dangerous things in the night.

"Are you certain that your boon is to know who I am?" he asked me.

I nodded.

"I had hoped to keep this from you a bit longer since you don't know," he admitted, "It's nice to meet someone who is interested in me without knowing my title."

"I'm pretty sure women are interested in you for more than your title," I said huskily.

He smiled down at me and then it wilted. "Will you tell me what you are?"

"I'm…" I hesitated. I needed to tell him the lie I had been using, but I didn't want to. He was the first person besides Emily that I didn't want to lie to.

"You're afraid," he whispered in shock.

"I would rather you get to know me more first," I admitted to him. "Please."

"You think what you are might drive me away?" he asked in shock. He smiled and shook his head. "Tora, I don't care what you are or what you used to be."

He said that now, but his attitude would change when he found out. Being friends with me was one thing, but dating or mating with me was completely different.

"Will you still tell me who you are?" I requested.

He nodded. "It is your boon for my failure to protect you."

"Wait," I whispered. He stood still and I stood on tiptoe to kiss him on the lips. "No matter what, just know that I'm interested in you even if you're a poor boy from limbo or a king from a foreign nation. Titles don't mean anything to me."

He pulled me roughly against him and kissed me hard. After a moment, he pulled back and then stepped fully away from me so that the cold night air wrapped around me again. "My full name is Edan Shaw, Prince of the Dragons."

The Dragon Prince! Holy cherubs on a stick. "The Prince?"

He nodded.

I had just kissed a prince. A real-life prince. Nice!

"Wow, I had no idea. I knew that someone said there was a prince at our school, but I had no idea it was the Dragon Prince, or that it was you."

"And?" he asked, walking closer to me.

"And what?" I asked as his warmth surrounded me again.

"That's all you have to say?" he asked.

"Why are you single?" I asked. "And seriously, how many girls have you had in that car? I think I might walk home. Your detailers have surely missed a spot or two."

He laughed at me and then pulled me against him and

kissed me. When he pulled back he looked at me with a serious expression and said, "Thank you for not caring."

"You're welcome."

"And just so you know, you don't have to hide what you are from me either."

Oh, yes, I did.

"Edan," I said with a sigh and started to pull away, but he held me fast.

"I'm not asking you to tell me today, but can you promise me that someday you will tell me?"

"Fine, if you and I are still together and things are serious in three weeks, I will tell you everything you want to know about me."

"Promise?"

"Promise," I said despite the fear thrumming through me.

We resumed our walk, holding hands and I wondered again at the familiarity I felt with him.

"A dragon?" I asked and stopped so suddenly that he stumbled a step.

"Yes."

"Can I see your true form?" I asked him excitedly.

"Maybe on our next date," he offered.

"So, there's going to be a next date?" I asked.

He squeezed our joined hands and said, "Contrary to the image of me that you have in your head, I do not date women often. You are a unique and interesting woman and I would very much like to continue seeing you."

"Are you saying that you are going to date me exclusively?" I asked in disbelief. A hot prince like him had his choice of women. Could he really want to exclusively date me after only two dates?

"I am. Is that something you are not willing to reciprocate?"

"Wait…" I said and paused. "You, Prince Edan, want to date me, Tora, exclusively? Like, boyfriend and girlfriend and you don't date or sleep with any other women?"

"And you don't date or sleep with any other men," he

agreed.

Wow.

"Uh…"

"You seem to be unsure."

"I'm just in shock and disbelief," I admitted.

"Tora, will you be my girlfriend?" he asked.

It sounded so silly and childish and yet it made me want to yell victoriously at the same time. "Yes."

He kissed me deeply and whispered, "Now, I'm definitely the luckiest male alive."

"Well, you do have me as a girlfriend," I said and brushed off my sleeve as though I were bragging.

Things were moving incredibly fast and although I didn't understand it, I wasn't opposed to it.

"What's it like to be Prince?" I asked while we continued our walk.

"Demanding and stressful at times. Boring and rewarding at others," he replied.

"What's your family like?"

"My mother is a fierce warrior who likes to charge into battle without a plan. My father is a calm and kind man who prefers strategy and negotiations to battle. They balance each other out and make for a great ruling pair."

"Your mom sounds fun," I said with a smirk.

He looked down at me and said, "I think you two would get along very well, as long as you didn't kill each other."

"You have no idea how many times I have heard that," I said with a sigh.

"What about your parents?" he asked. I froze a moment and he noticed. "Tora," he whispered and stopped me to face him, "What's wrong?"

"Sorry," I whispered, "My mother was a very gentle person and all she ever wanted was to sit in her flower garden."

"Was?" he asked gently.

"She was murdered two years ago," I explained.

"By who?"

"A woman who wants my father, but knew that he was in

love with my mother even though they were apart. She thought that by killing my mother she would have a shot with him."

"Is she still alive?" he asked and I saw the fierceness in his expression, the one that let me know that he was very loyal to his family.

"For now," I answered. "She's managed to evade me, but soon enough I'll track her down."

"What is your father like?" he asked and resumed walking.

"Terrifying, fierce, and incredibly powerful," I whispered and then shuddered as I recalled the weight of his power and how much pain he could inflict with hardly any effort.

"Perhaps I know him," he said.

"You definitely know of him," I mumbled. "How are you making the heat?" I asked to change the subject.

"This is my standard body temperature," he explained, "but most are not able to handle so much heat, so I shield it."

"That's got to take a lot of your magic away to shield your heat and shield your magic at the same time," I said and looked over at him.

He smiled. "It takes more than I would like, but I have plenty of reserves."

Just how powerful was he?

"No, I'm not going to fight you," he said before I could ask it.

"Oh, come on! I want to see *you*."

He dipped his head down next to my ear and whispered, "I think it's a bit early in our relationship for that."

"Scared?" I asked him.

"Of you? No. I am scared that I might lose control and burn down this city because I will be enjoying myself too much with you," he said and kissed the side of my neck.

"Sir!" a man yelled from next to us.

Edan and I both had our hands out, mine covered in lightning and his covered in fire and aimed at the man who had popped into existence beside us.

The man bowed. "I didn't mean to startle you both."

Edan looked at my hand and then me in shock before he

turned to the man. "What is it, Castille?"

"There's a minotaur army headed this way," he said and walked closer to us. "I've been ordered to bring you home."

Edan shook his head. "I'm not leaving her in danger."

"Minotaurs? Thor's hammer, it's been almost a decade since I fought one of those. How many are coming?" I asked Castille.

"More than twenty, but less than fifty was the head count I was given," he said. He turned to Edan. "We must leave now. I will teleport you and then come back and get her."

"No, teleport her first," Edan said.

"No way!" I argued and stepped away from them both. "I'm not letting you have all the fun. You're going to let him take me somewhere and then you're going to fight the minotaurs without me."

"I have no intention of fighting them. I only want you to get to safety," he said and started to walk closer to me.

"I don't need safety," I snapped. "I am not defenseless."

"All the same, I'd like to know that my girlfriend is out of harm's way," he growled at me.

"Sir?" Castille asked and glanced behind me nervously. The minotaurs were approaching fast. The ground shook beneath our feet from their heavy hooves and the water rippled beside us.

"I know that you are strong," Edan said to me, "but now is not the time to fight over this."

"No, now is the time for you to die," a deep male voice said behind me.

I spun around and used my lightning to electrocute the minotaur behind me. His body fell to the ground and then Edan grabbed me and pulled me into his arms. "Can we go now?" he asked.

The minotaur army was in front of us now and they were not happy about me killing one of them.

"But look at all the fun!" I insisted and waved towards the charging army.

"Finally found a girl like you, I see," Castille grumbled.

"Bring a mage back with you so that you can teleport us both out at the same time," Edan ordered Castille who disappeared the next moment.

Edan looked down at me and I saw the fire growing in his eyes. "As soon as they get back, we're leaving."

I nodded. "Deal." I stepped away from him and released some of my magic, letting my shield open a crack so I could access it. The power washed over me in a warm caress that made me sigh in happiness. I was faster, stronger, and deadlier with my magic. My ears also became pointed without my father's power being used.

"Elf?" Edan asked in shock.

"Only a quarter," I said. "Sword," I ordered my talisman, the bracelet on my right arm. It transformed into a black blade with a red hilt.

"That is definitely not elvish," he commented about my sword.

"Nope," I agreed and pointed it towards the minotaurs. "Who is your leader?"

"We aren't here for you, girl. We're here for him," one of the minotaurs in the front said.

I looked at Edan and asked, "What did you do to piss them off?"

He shrugged. "No clue."

"Kill them!" a minotaur bellowed.

The other minotaurs yelled in response and charged towards us.

"You going to participate?" I asked Edan who hadn't released any of his power yet.

"No, I think I'll watch you," he replied and leaned against a tree to my left.

I shrugged. "Suit yourself."

The first minotaur approached and I ran forward to meet him, my blade sliding through his upper body and cutting him in half before he even knew what hit him. I sliced through the minotaurs, one after the next until my sword was slippery with their blood. "Necklace," I ordered my talisman and stood in the center of the minotaurs. They formed a circle around me and I felt Edan's magic releasing.

"I don't know who you are, but you will pay for harming our brothers," a minotaur to my right snarled at me.

"Don't interrupt," I ordered Edan who was marching towards us.

"Pull your weapon out," he growled at me.

"No."

"This is not the time to be egotistical. I do not need you to impress me," he growled.

"Calm down," I whispered and smiled at him.

Castille and another mage appeared next to Edan and he looked at me pointedly.

"Fine, I'll finish this." I inhaled and then slammed my hands into the ground by my feet. Lightning shot out of my hands through the ground and electrocuted all of the minotaurs. They fell to the ground and I stepped around their bodies until I was in front of Edan. I inhaled, sealed up my shield and smiled at him. "All done."

"Who is that?" the newcomer asked. She was in her early to mid-twenties, tall and thin, but I could sense power from her.

"Isha," Edan said, "I would like you to meet my girlfriend, Tora."

"Girlfriend!" she screeched.

"Sir, your parents want you to return to them," Castille said.

"I can take, *Tora*, home if you'd like," Isha offered though she failed at hiding her disdain for me from her voice.

"You are dismissed," Edan ordered her.

"Edan," she whispered softly and took a step closer to him.

"Is there something wrong with your hearing?" Edan asked her and growled.

"Sir, there's something *dark* about her. I don't think it wise for you to be alone with her," she whispered to him.

I wasn't certain how she could see my darkness, but I was more focused on the obvious fact that she wanted him.

"You forget your place," Edan snapped at her.

She cringed and then bowed to him before she disappeared.

"I will escort Tora home and then I will return to speak to my parents," he informed Castille.

"You could bring her to meet them," Castille offered.

"No!" I said a bit too loud. "Not yet," I amended.

"She's right, it is too soon for her to meet them," Edan said with a smirk.

Castille bowed and disappeared.

"An army of minotaurs doesn't faze you, but the thought of meeting my parents does?" he asked me.

"I know where I stand with the minotaurs. The King and Queen of the Dragons, not so much."

"Are you afraid that they won't approve of you?" he asked and all humor drained out of him.

I didn't want to answer him. Of course they wouldn't approve of me. Once he found out what I was and who my father was, it was over.

"Tora," he chastised, "My parents may be the rulers of the Dragons, but they do not get to decide who I date."

"Can we continue our walk? It's starting to smell," I requested. It really was starting to smell from the minotaurs' bodies.

We resumed walking, his hand holding mine.

"Isha seems to have a crush on you," I commented.

He sighed. "I know."

"You know that if you had let her take me home that she would have tried to fight me?"

"Yes, which is why I didn't let her. I didn't want to explain to my family why she was dead and why I had to buy you a present in apology."

"A present? Maybe I should have accepted," I teased him.

"Can you promise me something?" he asked.

"Maybe," I said hesitantly.

"Next time there's some type of danger, let me handle it."

"Fine, next time it's your turn. We can swap," I said with a bright smile.

"It's my job to protect you. That's what the male is supposed to do," he argued.

"Does your dad protect your mom?" I asked.

He opened his mouth, closed it, and then growled. "That's different."

"Our relationship is only going to work if you learn to compromise," I said and looked up to see his reaction.

His anger disappeared to be replaced by surprise and then he smiled. "Our relationship. I like how that sounds."

"Weirdo," I teased.

We finally made it back to his car and when we slid inside I felt very tired. I yawned and leaned my head against his shoulder. "What time is it?"

"A bit after midnight," he answered.

"What? Where did the time go?" I swore we hadn't finished eating that long ago.

He put his arm around my shoulders and pulled me closer to him so that my head rested on his chest. "I'll take you home."

"Mm," I managed to say as I fell asleep on him.

I woke up as Edan carried me towards my dorm room. Girls lined the hallway and watched as I was carried by a Prince to my dorm. My face was hidden so none of them knew that I had woken up yet and Edan hadn't noticed either so I closed my eyes again. I opened them quickly when I heard the door shut behind us.

"Hey," I said and stretched in his arms. Having a man who could support my weight easily was definitely nice. "Sorry I fell asleep."

He looked at the two doors to the bedrooms and asked, "Which one is yours?"

I struggled to get out of his hold and standing. "Uh, the one on the left."

"I was going to carry you to your bed," he said with a smirk.

"It's a bit early for that," I said and smoothed down my shirt so I didn't have to look at him.

"Are you feeling alright?" he asked with concern.

"I've been abnormally tired the past couple days," I

admitted.

"I should leave you to rest then," he said and headed towards the door.

"And get to your family," I added.

He turned and said, "If you asked me to stay, I would make them wait."

"Perhaps another night," I said nervously. "We've already moved this relationship along faster than I normally would." I walked up to him and kissed him lightly on the lips. "I had a good time tonight."

"Do you have plans tomorrow?" he asked. He slid one hand around my side, just above my hip, and pulled me closer to him.

"I'm afraid so," I said with a sigh, lying.

"Oh?"

"My boyfriend is going to come over," I told him.

"Your what?" he growled. "You said…"

I looked up at him innocently and asked, "Aren't you coming over tomorrow?"

He laughed and bent down to whisper, "I'm going to get you back for that."

"Tease," I growled at him.

He nipped my neck, a zing of his power hitting the spot at the same time and my knees buckled. He held me up and whispered, "I can't wait to see you tomorrow."

I followed him out into the hall where the girls were still gathered, whispering in disbelief about Edan being here. He noticed them as well and gave me a glorious and over the top kiss in front of them all. He walked halfway down the hallway, spun around, bowed, and said, "Until tomorrow, my love."

I waved at him, dumbfounded by his overacting. Once he was gone all of the girls turned to look at me. I giggled girlishly and skipped into my dorm where I promptly went to bed.

CHAPTER THREE

Emily was gone the entire day, which I was fairly certain was on purpose, but since Edan was over I didn't care. He arrived early with donuts and hot chocolate. Instead of tight clothing, he wore sweatpants and a sweatshirt.

"You're rather casual today," I commented as I chewed my donut. I made sure that I was fully dressed, teeth brushed, and hair brushed before he made it over.

"It's my one day off," he explained, "Today I do not have any Prince duties and have turned my cell off."

"And you chose to spend it with me?" I asked. "I feel so honored."

"You should," he said and nodded. "I don't normally leave the castle on my days off."

"Why?" Didn't he have friends?

"Leaving the castle means running into groupies," he muttered.

"Such a rough life you have," I mocked him.

His lip lifted in a snarl and he lunged for me. I was halfway across the living room before he made it to the couch. "You're pretty fast," he commented and smiled as he began to stalk me around the room.

"You should see how fast I am when I'm using my

powers," I teased him.

"Now who is the tease?" he asked with a smirk.

"So, what do you want to do? Since it's your day off, I'll let you choose."

He pinned me against the wall and I gasped in shock. I'd barely seen him move. He kissed me deeply, his arms around me to keep our bodies pressed together. "How about we watch a movie and then we can go out to lunch somewhere?"

I grabbed him by the back of the neck and pulled his face to mine, kissing him again. Damn he was an amazing kisser. "Sounds good," I said breathlessly.

I started to walk back to the couch, but he scooped me up and tossed me over his shoulder. I screamed in fake terror and hit his back with closed fists gently. "Put me down you brute!" I said in a high-pitched voice.

He chuckled and then tossed me on the couch. He went to pin me down, but I wrapped my legs around his waist and spun him around so that he ended up on his back on the couch and I sat on him. "This was not the plan," he mumbled, but was still smiling.

"I had to make sure that you couldn't reach the remote," I lied and picked up the controller. "You seem like someone who would want to watch a classic movie."

"What's wrong with classics?" He slid his hand up and down my lower leg.

"They're perfect for naps, but I'd rather watch something a bit more interesting." Despite my plan to keep the shenanigans to a low level, I leaned forward and kissed him again. He slid his hands along each side of my face, pushing my hair back and turned his head to kiss me deeper.

When we finally separated, I climbed off of him and found a movie for us to watch. He put his arm around my shoulders and we watched the movie. I let him pick the next one and we realized that we had a lot of common interests.

"What do you want for lunch?" he asked.

"How about pizza? We can get it delivered so you don't have to deal with groupies," I offered.

He twirled a strand of my hair around his finger and said, "I think going out will be good. That way they can see me with you and know I'm off the market."

"Hopefully none of them has figured out how to make someone's head explode from glaring."

He laughed and kissed my cheek. "I'll protect you."

"It seems like I'll actually be protecting you from their attention."

He smirked. "True."

"Give me one minute," I requested. I went to my bathroom and brushed my hair and checked my makeup. I didn't wear much makeup, but since we were bound to get a lot of attention, I wanted to have some eye shadow and eye liner on at the very least.

"Hello sexy," Edan said.

"Ready?" I asked.

He dipped me to the side and kissed me. "Now I am."

As soon as we walked out of my dorm, the stares began. Edan draped his arm across my shoulders and led me outside.

"What would you like for lunch?" he asked me.

How could he stand all of these people staring at him?

"I'll eat pretty much anything," I replied.

"Who is she?"

"She isn't even that attractive."

"He could do so much better."

Wow, these girls were vicious.

Must. Not. Obliterate.

"I think your pizza suggestion is sticking with me. How about a pizza?"

"Sounds great."

We walked through the college grounds and it was not an exaggeration to say that every single person looked at us as we went by.

"Have I told you today how beautiful you are?" he asked.

I looked up at him just as he bent and kissed me.

That sent them all squawking.

"No, I don't think you have," I replied with a smug smile.

He twirled some of my hair around his finger and said, "You are the most beautiful woman in the world. Your beauty would make Aphrodite weep with jealousy."

"Oh, what a silver tongue you have."

He leaned closer and whispered, "I think you'll fall in love with my tongue soon."

"Oh, tease," I purred.

He pushed open the door to the pizza place and pushed me towards an open booth. I took a seat in the booth and watched him place our order. Even in sweatpants you could see the muscles in his legs. How much could he squat? His shoulders stretched his sweatshirt and made my stomach and other parts squirm a bit.

If only mating wasn't such a serious thing for non-humans. I really wanted a taste of him.

"You're blushing," he whispered. He set down a mug of beer in front of me and leaned back.

"How do you stand the attention?" I asked instead of responding to his comment.

"I ignore it."

"How? The comments and stares are pissing me off and it's only been an hour."

He slid his hand across the table to lace our fingers together. "I'm sorry. Would you prefer if we got the pizza to go?"

"That's not what I meant," I mumbled. "I just don't understand how you don't respond to their comments."

"Sometimes it's hard. Especially today when they were talking about you," he admitted. "I just have to remember that I'm expected to act a certain way and beating up everyone who said something I didn't like would result in me being locked up for the rest of my life."

"Maybe beating up a few of them would get them to stop," I suggested.

He smiled. "I think you just want to see me in a fight."

It was my turn to smile. "I would enjoy that, but that's not why I'm suggesting it."

"Who would you like me to fight?" he asked and leaned forward conspiratorially. "Is there an ex-boyfriend you'd like me to rough up?"

I fought not to cringe at the reminder of my ex, but he must have seen it. "No, but if I figure out someone I will let you know."

He squeezed my hand and asked, "Do you want to talk about it?"

"No, not really."

"What's your favorite weapon?" he asked me.

"I don't have a favorite," I admitted. "I like swords, axes, and really every weapon equally. They all have their own uses."

"It seems to me that you prefer not even using a weapon."

"Why use a weapon when I'm already one?" I asked with as much innuendo as I could.

His eyes flared with power, but he quickly tamped it down. "Tease."

"Promise."

Our pizza came and I found it easier to forget the stares and just talk with him. He was easy to be around and I felt incredibly comfortable with him even though I hadn't known him long.

After pizza, he walked me back to my dorm and then gave me one hell of a kiss bye. He promised to come back later, so I went to take a nap.

* * *

"You have a guest," Emily called through my door.

"Sleepy," I mumbled without moving.

My door opened a moment later and then someone sat on my bed.

"Em, I'm tired," I complained and pushed at her body, but the usually soft body of Emily was instead hard and muscular. "Who?" I asked but didn't have the energy to sit up.

"Tora," Edan's voice said. "You need to wake up."

"What time is it? Why are you here so early?" I complained.

"This has happened several days now," Emily said from somewhere in my room.

"Did you scan her?" Edan asked Emily.

"No, I thought she was just tired."

"This isn't a normal tired. We weren't out that late the night before and she's had more than enough sleep."

"We need lots of sleep," I complained.

"We?" he asked.

"She means her kind," Emily answered, which I was grateful for because I almost gave it away.

"This is too much for any race," he argued. "Please, open your eyes."

I reluctantly obeyed and found him frowning down at me. "Serious face," I mumbled.

"How do you feel?" he asked and set his hand on my forehead.

"Tired," I answered and yawned. I slapped a hand over my mouth when I realized that I likely had bad breath and I had just breathed it on my new boyfriend. "I'm going to go to the restroom."

He let me stand up and began whispering with Emily. When I finished brushing my teeth and hair and freshening up, I came out to find her looking nervous as he scowled at her.

"What's going on?" I asked them.

"Nothing," Emily said and smiled at me. "Come here, let me have a look at you."

I waved her off. "I'm fine. I used some of my magic last night to fight some minotaurs, so it's probably from that."

"It didn't sound like you used much based on Edan's retelling," she countered.

"No, I used very little, but…"

She froze me in place and began using her magic to scan me.

I growled at her and struggled against the freezing spell.

"I didn't know you could do that," Edan whispered and walked around me.

"Stop growling," she ordered me. She finished her scan and

looked at Edan. "Do you want the good news or the bad news first?"

"Why does he get to pick!" I yelled.

"Good," he replied.

"She's not dead."

"Obviously!" I screamed and threw my hands up into the air, glad she finally released me.

"What's the bad news?" he asked.

I paced back and forth and grumbled. "I'm right here. I know they can see me. Rude."

"She's dying."

I stopped and spun to face her. "Come again?"

"It's a slow acting spell that steals the being's strength and power, funneling it into a container, until the being has no power left and withers away."

"Can you tell who cast it?" Edan asked.

"No, but I know what race," she said and then looked at me sadly.

"No," I whispered. "He wouldn't."

"You know it's almost impossible for people to break their contracts," she whispered.

"It's broken."

"But if he is the only one who can save your life, what type of contract would you be willing to sign for that?" she asked.

She had to be right. I didn't doubt it for a moment.

"A demon is doing this?" Edan asked angrily.

"Yes," Emily replied.

"Will the spell's process speed up if I go to the demon realm?" I asked even though I knew the answer.

"Yes. You'll be dead within minutes."

"You are *not* going to the demon realm," Edan growled.

"You could always ask *him* for help," Emily suggested.

"Are you crazy!" I yelled and began pacing. "Do you have any idea what I would have to do for him to help me? I wouldn't be able to leave the demon realm for a hundred years. A contract with Beel would be a thousand times better than a contract with *him*."

"Beel, that's who your contract was with?" Edan asked.

Uh oh. "Edan, this is not your concern," I said gently. "I will handle this."

"You promised," he whispered.

"That does not apply to the current situation. That was a promise that if a griffin started attacking us, I would let you handle it. Not that I would let you handle this!"

"What are you planning to do?" he asked.

"I'm going to summon him and find out if it is really him or not." I had other enemies so it could be any number of people.

"I'll compromise with you," he said softly, but with folded arms that made me think this wouldn't be much of a compromise. "I'll allow you to handle it, but I want to be here with you when you summon him."

That could go wrong in so many ways. "He's not going to like you being with me," I told him.

"Are we together or not? If we're together then you shouldn't have a problem telling him," Edan said.

I looked at Emily for help. Once Beel found out that I was dating someone, he would get the information to my dad and I had no clue what he would do, if anything.

"I agree with Edan," she said.

"Traitor," I grumbled.

"How long does she have if the spell continues to progress at the rate that it is?" Edan asked her.

"Four weeks."

"Perfect," I said, "I'll summon him in three weeks."

"What?" Edan asked in shock.

"Why do you want to wait that long?" Emily asked me.

"Edan and I have an agreement that I'll reveal my race and who my father is if we're still together in three weeks and our relationship is serious," I informed her.

"If he speeds it up at all, you could be dead before then," Emily said softly.

"He won't. If this really is him, then he'll enjoy the game."

"What if it's not him?" Edan asked.

I looked at Emily and said, "Then I'll call my father."

"I don't like this plan," Edan growled and paced back and forth in our tiny living room.

"If you let me meet with Beel alone, I could do it today," I said and shrugged. "Your call."

"Why don't you want me to be here?" he asked. "Are you afraid that I'll see something between you two? Wait, is he your father?"

I laughed and then shook my head. "Beel is not my father and I already told you that there is nothing between us. I don't want you here because I'm likely going to need to use my full power to attack him."

"All the more reason for me to be here, as back up."

"She doesn't want you to see her change," Emily told him.

"Emily!" I gasped.

"Change? What do you mean?"

"That's not her true form."

"Emily, shut up. This is not your place."

She marched over to me and we stood with our faces inches apart while we yelled.

"I refuse to let my friend die because she's scared of getting dumped!" she snapped.

"It's not just that and you know it!" I yelled back at her.

She waved her hand at Edan and said, "He's not going to kill you!"

"He might try!" I yelled.

"He won't!"

"How do you know?" I asked.

"Look at him," she ordered me. I glanced over to see him watching us with concern. "Does he look like he's going to kill you?"

"He doesn't know," I whispered. "When he does, he could change."

"Why do you think he'll change so drastically?" Emily asked. "What are you so afraid of?"

"I don't want to hurt him! I don't want to kill another man that I love to protect myself!" I yelled at her.

Her mouth opened in shock and Edan dropped his arms to

his side in disbelief. I clamped a hand over my mouth and ran out of the dorm, down the hall, and out into the busy campus. I was in my pajamas, but I didn't care. I needed to get away. I needed to find someplace abandoned. People stared at me with curiosity, but then they looked up into the sky. What were they looking at? I didn't have time to look.

I made it all the way to the park on the side of the school where students were lying in the grass, reading, or playing sports. My progress was halted by Edan dropping out of the sky in front of me, wings flared out on either side of him, he landed with one hand on the ground and looked up at me.

"I'm sorry," I whispered, "I can't. I need…"

I backed away from him, trying to escape, but people had formed a circle around us, drawn by his presence, especially with his wings out.

"Stop running," he ordered me and folded his wings in behind him.

Lightning fizzled down my arms. I tucked my hands in my arm pits and backed up. "Stay back," I ordered him weakly.

"Tora," he whispered softly. "Calm down."

Lightning crackled around me and people gasped in fear. They backed up, but were too curious to leave.

"You should leave," I told him. "I swear, I won't hold it against you or…"

He flew across the distance between us, faster than I thought he could move, grabbed me and flew us up into the sky. I latched onto his neck and calmed myself to prevent from hurting him with my lightning.

"Will you tell me what happened?" he asked calmly as he flew us high into the sky above the school.

"He found out and tried to kill me," I whispered. "Not much else to tell."

"Do you truly believe that I would try to kill you?" he asked and nuzzled my neck with his nose.

"Yes."

He jerked his head back and looked at my face a long moment. "You have much to learn about me."

"Ditto," I whispered and then sniffed as I fought not to cry.

"Do you have wings in your true form?" he asked.

"Why?"

"Because you aren't afraid of flying and from what I've heard from other dragons, most are terrified of flying the first time."

"Yes," I whispered.

"Yes, you have wings?" he asked.

I nodded.

"Will you show me them sometime?" he asked.

"In three weeks," I offered.

He sighed, but didn't say more about the subject. He landed in front of a large castle and I recoiled. The Dragon castle. "Why are we here?"

He gripped my shoulders and said, "I'm going to find someone to help you."

"Edan, I…"

"Ho, there!" a male yelled as he jogged down the stairs towards us. He was short and stocky and had a smile that was infectious.

"Isaac," Edan greeted.

"I saw you flying in so I thought I'd come meet you." He stopped when he reached the last few steps and noticed me. "Oh, hello."

"Isaac, this is my girlfriend, Tora."

"Girlfriend!" he yelled.

Edan slipped his arm around my waist and I noticed that his wings were gone now. I also noticed that his hold was a bit tighter than normal. He was probably worried that I might run off again.

"Sorry, I lost my manners for a moment." He bowed and said, "Nice to meet you, Tora. I am Isaac, Prince Edan's assistant."

"Assistant?" I asked Edan.

"Like a valet. He helps me with my schedule and other things."

"Your mother has requested that you see her immediately," Isaac informed him.

Edan started to move forward, but I pulled back, towards the gates. "Tora," he chastised.

"Too soon," I whispered around the lump in my throat. I continued backing up, but Edan kept his hand on my waist and walked back with me.

"She's going to love you. Come on. You don't need to be frightened."

"I can't...what happens when they find out?" I asked him.

"What's up?" Isaac asked.

"A moment please," Edan requested. Isaac walked up the stairs some ways away from us. "I know you have darkness in you, Tora. I can sense it and could from the moment I met you. I don't care. I don't care what you are or who you are related to. I care that you make me happy. I care that you don't see me for my title or money. I care that you see *me*. You are the first girl to see me, ever. I can deal with your baggage and I swear to never harm you."

"If she attacks me..."

"If she attacks you, I will defend you," he swore.

"It's too soon," I whispered.

"You said it," he whispered back.

I had hoped he hadn't heard that.

"You told me that you loved me."

"I meant..."

"You're mine now. I won't give you up and I don't care what you say about your past or race. Do you understand?"

"I'm yours?" I asked.

He nodded and touched his fingertip to the spot on my neck he had bit last night. "You're marked."

"What!" I yelled. "You didn't tell me."

"That's what I had planned to do today when I came over."

"It's not right," I whispered. "These feelings shouldn't be happening so soon."

"But they are for us both," he whispered.

"Wait." I looked up at him. "Both?"

He kissed me and then rested his forehead against mine. "You and I are going to go somewhere far away and have a very long discussion after we see my parents. Okay?"

That sounded wonderful. "Okay."

We walked up to Isaac who was waiting patiently and he smiled at me. "Ready?"

"No," I grumbled, but Edan simply laughed at me.

He linked our hands together and we walked up the giant staircase carved from some type of gorgeous rock, and into a giant castle made from the same white stone.

Servants bustled about, but everyone stopped to stare when they saw us.

"Why are they staring?" I asked.

"They've never seen Prince Edan with a lady before. Many presumed he would never marry," Isaac explained.

"He's not very old," I commented. "Why would they think that?"

"Dragons typically find their mates by their twentieth birthday," Isaac said.

"Wait, I'm not a dragon," I said and looked at Edan.

He shrugged. "It doesn't matter. If I become King, I won't need you to be a dragon, just strong enough to fight beside me as a Queen."

King? Queen? Oh boy.

Isaac opened the doors to a large, empty room save for some pillows along the base of the walls where a few women were lounging. They looked up at our entry and stood.

"Prince Edan," they all said at the same time in greeting.

Creepy.

"Son? Is that you?" a woman called from outside the double doors at the end of the room, which led to a balcony. She walked into the room and I stared in disbelief. She was tall, muscular for a woman, and yet drop dead gorgeous. She also radiated power like Edan did.

She looked at me and our joined hands and her eyes narrowed. "What is this?"

"Mother, this is Tora, my girlfriend."

"Girlfriend? You've never brought her to us before," she said and walked towards me.

"I didn't see a need to," he said nonchalantly.

"Where did you meet?"

"School."

"Tora, that means thunder, doesn't it?"

"Yes, Your Majesty," I replied awkwardly.

"Come, let me see you," she ordered.

Edan nudged me forward and I strode towards her confidently despite my worry.

"Hm, I can see why he likes you. Are you a fighter, dear?"

"Yes."

Without warning she threw a dagger at my face. I caught it between my pointer and middle fingers and she clapped. "Marvelous!"

"Mother!" Edan growled.

"She caught it, don't get so mad," she told him.

"Where's Ingrid?" Edan asked.

"In the healer's quarters. Why?" she asked suspiciously. She looked over at me and asked, "Are you pregnant?"

"No!" I yelled. "We haven't mated." What kind of girl did she think I was!

She smiled and then I felt her magic probing at mine. I stepped back from her, dropping the dagger as I moved towards Edan. "Stop," I begged.

"Lift your shields," she ordered and slammed her magic into my shield.

"Enough," Edan growled at her.

She didn't stop. A crack formed along my shield and I tried to repair it. She hit me with her magic again and I fell to the ground. If she were my enemy, I would have killed her instantly, but I could not harm her.

"Enough!" Edan bellowed and let his magic out in a tidal wave of pure power.

His mother staggered a step back and gasped. "Edan…"

"Leave her alone," he ordered her and then picked me up.

"What are you?" she asked me. "You're not a dragon and

you're not human."

"She's mine and I would appreciate it if you wouldn't attack her again," Edan growled.

He walked out of her chambers with Isaac right on his heels. "Do you think that was wise?" Isaac asked him.

Edan glared at him and continued on his way.

"You can set me down. I can walk," I told him.

His fingers gripped my sides and he didn't respond. Alright, I guess I was getting carried. We walked into a white room that was sterile and smelled funny.

"Demons!" A man yelled as he ran down the hallway.

What?

"How many?" Edan asked.

"An army!" the man snapped. "At least two hundred."

"Who is leading them?" I asked and pushed myself out of Edan's arms to stand.

"I...I don't know," the man said, surprised to see me.

I headed towards the way we had come in so I could get out. Between the Queen attacking my shields and now, Beel had slowed the spell down so I was able to regain my normal power.

"Where do you think you are going?" Edan growled.

"I'm going to have a word with the demon army," I said as I continued walking.

"You are not in any condition..." he began, but I interrupted him with a jolt of electricity.

"The spell was slowed. I can't explain this, but I need to go confront them so that they don't cause any damage to this realm," I explained.

I stepped outside and was shocked to see an army of dragons, some in dragon form and others in human form, gathered to fight the demons. Increasing my speed, I began to run in the direction everyone was looking. "Tell them to stand down!" I yelled at Edan who had been stopped by an older man that looked exactly like him and I had no doubt was his father. "I can handle this without any of you needing to be involved."

Edan said something to his dad while snarling in my direction. If I could convince them to leave without needing to reveal who I was to them, I could keep my secret a bit longer. The army finally came into view and my eyes widened at the number of demons gathered. Why were so many here? At the front of the army was Arton, a very low level demon who was always causing trouble.

"I should have known," I grumbled and hurried towards them.

The army stopped and Arton stepped to the front and roared at me.

"Pathetic!" I screamed at him.

He flinched and snarled at me. "What do you want, human?"

I rolled my eyes. Even though I was in a different form, he should have sensed that I was a demon. "Go back to the Demon Realm immediately!" I ordered them.

The dragons approached behind me in formation with Edan and his parents at the lead. I needed to get the demons out of here now.

"Who do you think you are?" Arton growled.

I let a bit of my demonic power out and allowed my eyes to change into their true shape and color. "Leave or I will punish you," I threatened them.

A few demons rushed forward and I electrocuted them immediately. Arton charged at me, but Beel appeared in front of him and stopped him. Beel said something to him and Arton's eyes widened. "That can't be her," he snarled at Beel.

Beel said something again to him and Arton said, "I don't care. I'm moving forward."

Beel turned towards me and smiled. "Unless you reveal who you really are, they won't leave."

"Let us handle this," Edan called to me and moved forward.

I put up an invisible wall between the dragons and us. Edan ran into it and snarled. "I'm sorry," I said as I turned to face him. "I should have told you the truth. You were right, I am scared of your reaction." I looked at his parents. "And your family's reaction. I can't help what I was born as."

"I don't care what you are," Edan told me. "Break this wall and let me help you."

"This is one time that you can't help me," I said. "If you decide that you don't wish to continue our relationship, please just let me leave after this. I don't want to hurt you."

"Tora," he called softly. "Please."

"Kill her!" Arton yelled.

The army began to move forward, shouting and releasing their powers. It was now or never. Inhaling deep, I released the restraints I had placed on myself and my shape and allowed my true self to come through. It felt like breaking out of an egg. My horns grew from my head, my tail slit a hole in my pants, and smoke poured out of my nostrils. My eyes were glowing as was my entire body.

I opened my eyes and felt free for the first time in a very long time. "Return to the Demon Realm by my order!" I bellowed at the demons.

Several turned tail and ran as soon as they realized who I was. Arton stood, dumbstruck with his mouth open.

"Both of you as well," I snarled at Arton and Beel.

"I don't care who you are!" Arton bellowed. "I will complete my mission!"

"You dare to challenge me!" I bellowed back.

"You don't frighten me!" he snarled.

"How about me? Do I frighten you?" The deepest male voice I had ever heard asked.

"King!" some of the lesser demons who had stayed gasped.

"You dare to challenge your Princess?" Father asked as he came to stand next to me.

"I can handle this," I assured him.

"I know you can, but I have been on the sidelines too long. Sometimes the king must come and remind his subjects why they fear him. This should last us at least ten years," he explained.

"What are you going to do, kill us?" Arton asked haughtily.

"For challenging your Princess, I claim all of your souls for eternity!" Dad bellowed. He flicked his finger and every demon fell, except for Arton and Beel. "Would you clean the field up?" Dad asked me.

"Yes, Father," I said and with one exhale engulfed all of the bodies in white fire. They turned to ash an instant later.

"Arton, you've been a nuisance lately, but I think you just need some retraining," Father said. "To the pit with you," he ordered and snapped his finger. Arton disappeared leaving Beel alone.

"You can't kill me," Beel said smugly.

"Oh?" Father asked. "Why would you say that?"

"Because if you kill me, she dies," Beel told him with a wide smile.

Father turned to look at me and growled angrily. He grasped me by the arm. "You're dying, you idiot. Why didn't you summon me?" He pointed at me and I froze in place. "They always tell you that children are stupid, but you have surpassed all of my wildest dreams."

Fire engulfed my chest, but I refused to cry or scream. A moment later it was gone and so was Beel's spell, returning my full power to me.

"What! How?" Beel demanded.

Father set me so that I sat on the ground and smiled at Beel. "Did you think a spell like that would be difficult for me to break? Clearly, you have all forgotten how powerful I am."

I had not. I knew that he was the most powerful being in existence. He could destroy the world in a matter of minutes if he wanted to.

"She's mine!" Beel screamed.

Edan snarled, shattered my wall, and flew over to tackle Beel in his dragon form. His dragon form was glorious.

"A dragon?" Father asked. "What are the dragons doing here?"

Beel held his own for a bit, but Edan was too strong. "She's mine," Edan snarled at Beel and then killed him with one swipe of his claws.

"It's been a long time since I've killed dragons," Dad said excitedly.

I leapt up and let my powers out again. "You will not touch them!" I growled at him.

Dad smirked and asked, "Are you challenging me, Daughter? Do you want a test?"

"I'm stronger than the last time I challenged you," I assured him.

"Tora," Edan called from where he had returned next to his parents, but I put up a stronger wall this time that he could not break.

"Stay out of this," I ordered him.

He growled, but his mother grabbed his arm and said, "This is something she must do alone."

"Are you sure?" Father asked. "You know the penalty."

I roared at him as loudly as I could, the ground beneath me shook.

Father smirked and instantly pissed me off. "Don't laugh at my roar! I don't sound like that anymore!" I screamed.

"I'm sorry," he apologized, "but whenever you roar I will always hear the sound you made when you released your very first roar as a toddler."

"I'm not a child any longer. I'm an adult."

"A stupid one. How could you sign a contract with Beel?"

"It was better than what you wanted for me."

"Come, I grow weary of this place," he ordered me.

I sent electricity through the ground and fire from my mouth at him. He smiled proudly and then I was on the ground as he stood over me, unscathed.

"You have grown stronger, but you have a long way to go before you can stand up to me."

Dammit.

He grasped one of my horns and said, "You know the price."

I nodded. "Yes, Father."

"Stop!" Edan yelled.

"Would you like to take her place?" Father asked.

"Don't you dare touch him!" I screamed.

While looking at Edan, Father snapped the top half of my right horn off. It hurt worse than anything else could, but I would not cry or scream in front of my father. I could not show weakness.

"Tora!" Edan bellowed.

I took a shuddering breath as I lay on the ground, pain coursing from my horn throughout my entire body.

Edan charged forward, but Father easily caught him and held him on the ground a few feet away from me. "A dragon? The Prince of the Dragons even," Father said with a smile and looked at me. "Things are progressing quickly between the two of you, aren't they?"

"How'd you know?" I asked. How could he possibly know that?

"You're both creatures of fire and prince and princess."

"What does that have to do with anything?"

"Bonding is accelerated for royalty. I don't know why, but it is," Father said and shrugged. "I approve of this match."

"I don't need your approval," I snarled.

"Perhaps I should kill him to keep him from sidetracking you," Father suggested.

I stood up on shaky legs and stared straight into his eyes. "If you touch a single hair on him or any of the dragons, I will destroy the demon realm."

Father's eyes widened and then he beamed at me with pride in his dark eyes. "Come home with me."

"You have another heir," I reminded him. Though I had not seen D'marcus in many years.

"D'marcus is dead. I thought you knew," Father informed me.

"Dead? How?" I asked softly.

"Picked a fight he could not win. You, my dear, are heir once more."

"I don't want to be your heir. I don't want to run the Demon Realm."

"I need to return," Father told me. He looked down at

Edan and said, "Come see me in three days and bring the dragon."

"Yes, Father."

He disappeared and Edan rushed over to me as I collapsed from the pain of my horn. My wings disappeared as I fell.

"We need to get you to a healer."

"Just cauterize it," I ordered him.

"It will hurt."

"Just do it."

He took a deep breath and then blew fire across the top of my broken horn. I grunted from the pain and his grip on my shoulders tightened.

"I'm sorry," I whispered. "I shouldn't have tried to have a relationship with you."

"Why not?" he asked and pushed my hair away from my face.

"Because of who I am."

He shook his head and said, "I told you already that I don't care what you are and I meant it. I don't care that you're Princess of the Demons just like you don't care that I am Prince of the Dragons."

"What?" I asked in disbelief.

"Come on, let's get you to the healer," he said.

I stood up and leaned on him for support. "You're really not going to try to kill me?" I asked him.

He tilted my chin up and kissed me. "No. I will never hurt you."

"Prince Edan," Isha called as she walked towards us with flames on her hands. "Please, move away from the demon."

"You are out of line," Edan growled at her.

"Stand aside and let me kill her. The sooner we kill her, the safer we will all be."

"Isha, return to the castle," The King ordered her.

"Sir, I can…"

"That was an order, not a request."

She glared at me and then disappeared.

"I apologize. We should have fired her a long time ago,"

the King told me. He held out his hand. "I'm Elam."

I shook his hand and felt numb from shock. He'd protected me? "Tora."

"I've heard all about you," he assured me with a smile.

"Father," Edan growled.

"Come, join us for dinner," Elam offered.

"I don't know," I whispered and looked down at my tail which was draped across my right foot.

"Please," the Queen asked. "I have to make up for my misbehavior earlier."

"Please?" Edan asked softly.

It would not be a good thing to upset the rulers of the dragons, so I nodded my head in agreement.

"I'll meet you after I take her to the healer," Edan informed them.

I looked down at my pajamas. "I'm not exactly, um, dressed for dinner with your family."

"We'll make it a pajama party," the Queen said with a smile. "It will give me an excuse to wear pajamas early."

"Why?" I asked. "Why are you being so nice to a demon?"

"You're not a demon," Elam said, "You are our son's girlfriend."

"I told you they would like you," Edan whispered and then flew up into the air and glided towards the castle.

"Did you know royalty bonded faster?" I asked. His body was incredibly warm, which was comforting at the moment.

"Yes, my parents told me that. I assumed that meant you were royalty."

"You did?" I asked and looked up at him.

"I thought you might not know," he said and then smiled. "Obviously, you do though."

"I won't be able to switch forms for at least an hour," I mumbled in embarrassment.

"You're beautiful in either form," he whispered, kissed my neck where he had marked me, and exhaled loudly.

"I can't believe you marked me without asking," I grumbled.

"It's removable," he said, "and I wanted to be sure I could locate you."

"In case I ran away," I teased.

"Who would run away from this?" he asked and flexed the bicep on his left arm.

I laughed and shook my head. "Your ego is as big as your dragon form."

He dropped through an opening in the ceiling, right into the white, sterile room we had stepped into before the army had come. "Ingrid!" he called.

A blonde-haired woman with orange cat ears walked out of a nearby office. Her tail was orange and white striped and it swished behind her as she walked. "Prince," she greeted, "to what do I owe the pleasure of your visit?"

"She needs to be healed," he explained and set me on an empty table in what was their infirmary. The hole in the ceiling was a smart tactic for bringing their injured, but also a security risk.

"What if someone tries to break in through here?" I asked, face tilted up to look at the opening.

"Ingrid is more than capable of protecting the entrance," Edan explained.

Ingrid scanned my body and then placed her hand against my horn. "I can't heal this any more than it already is."

"Why not?" Edan asked.

"When the King of Demons punishes you, it must heal on its own," I explained.

"I'll tend to the minor wounds you have," she said and healed a few bruises on my arms and face that I had likely gained from Father pinning me to the ground.

"Thank you," I said to her and played with the end of my tail. It was triangle shaped, sharp, and convenient for fighting.

"You're welcome," she said, bowed, and then returned to her office.

"You're scowling," I said to Edan who had stood in silence beside me with a frown the entire time. "What's wrong?"

"If I take over as King of the Dragons and you have to rule

the Demon Realm as Queen, where does that leave us?"

"I'm never going to rule the demons," I assured him. "I'll find another heir for Father." I would create one if I had to.

"It is your birthright," he countered.

"I don't want to rule the demons," I said sincerely.

"And what about the dragons?" he asked.

"I'll leave that to you," I mumbled. "If we ever reach that point."

"By default, you would become Queen."

"Stop scaring the girl with such serious talk so soon in your relationship," his mother chastised him. "Come on, it's time for dinner."

"Give us a moment," he requested.

She nodded and left the room.

Uh oh.

Edan turned towards me and his serious frown turned into a smirk. "I'm sorry. I've always been told that I focus on serious things too often. I did not mean to frighten you by talking about a future which is far off."

"It's fine. These are things we have to think about before deciding to continue our relationship," I agreed.

"You forgive me?" he asked, picked my hands up and pulled me closer to him.

"I don't know," I said with a sigh. "Perhaps a gift might cheer me up?" I teased.

"A gift?" he asked and leaned forward, his lips close to mine. "Would you settle for a kiss?"

"A kiss from the Dragon Prince would likely sell for a lot at the college," I chuckled and leaned forward.

"You going to auction it off to the highest bidder?" he questioned with a smile.

Closing the gap, I pressed my lips to his and wrapped my arms around his neck. He wrapped his arms around my waist and my tail wrapped around his leg.

"They're all mine now," I whispered.

He rubbed his thumb across my lower lip and said, "Ditto."

"Children!" his mother called.

We laughed.

"Do you have long lifespans?" I questioned.

He nodded. "From what I know, the same as demons."

"Phew," I said and exhaled. "I thought I was going to have to deal with you being old and prune-y."

He bumped his hip into mine and tightened his grip on my hand. "Not for a very long time."

"Your fan club is going to be so sad," I chuckled.

He snorted. "Good. I'm so tired of them stalking me. Did you know that one of them actually cut a piece of my hair to keep? That's why I have the haircut I have now."

Currently it was spiked on top and had a fade shave on the sides. It did make it harder for them to cut his hair.

"Did she use it to perform a spell?" I wondered aloud.

He stopped walking. "I hadn't thought about that."

"It's a possibility."

He sighed. "Wonderful, one more thing to worry about."

I nudged his side with my elbow. "I've got your back."

He smiled and kissed my cheek as we walked towards a room with a lot of boisterous activity going on inside. "That is incredibly reassuring."

"No, 'ditto'?" I asked and feigned hurt.

He rolled his eyes. "That goes without saying."

My tail raised and slapped his butt cheek. He stopped walking and looked over at my tail.

"It has a mind of its own," I said in embarrassment.

He reached towards it, but I pulled it up to my chest and held it between my hands.

He held out his hand, palm up. "Please."

Never in my life had I let a male touch my tail. He hadn't tried to kill me when he found out I was a demon princess and had attempted to protect me from my father, so I had to assume he really did care for me. Slowly, I released my hold on it and let my tail fall into his waiting hand.

He stroked a finger down the top flat part, making me shudder and my eyelids droop. Holy lighting, that felt amazing. He turned my tail sideways and slid his finger tip down the side, cutting himself and drawing blood.

"It's sharp," I gasped and tried to pull it back.

"It's just a small cut," he whispered and showed me that it was already healing.

"I think I can change back," I said.

Shaking his head, he released my tail and pinned me to the wall with his arms on either side of my head. "I don't want you to change back yet. I'd like to have more time with you in this form."

"You haven't exactly had much time with me in the other form either," I said breathlessly. He was broad, muscular, and the sexiest male alive.

His nostrils flared and then he kissed me, pressing his body to mine, forcing my body against the stone wall. So much strength was coiled within his body, so much power and destructive capability. He was dangerous and I loved it.

He pulled back from our kiss and traced my pointed ear. "I'll have lots of time with your other form at school, so I'll take as much time with you in this one as I can."

"I want to see you in your other form," I said with a smirk and stroked my fingertip down his forearm beside my head.

"Plenty of time for that," he promised. His warm lips pressed against my neck and then over his mark. "Do I have your permission to mark you?" he asked and flicked his tongue across the mark.

"You already did," I reminded him.

"Yes or no?" he asked.

"Yes."

He bit down, his canines pierced my skin and drew blood. Magic pressed against my shields, warm and definitely his. I opened them to his magic and suddenly we were submerged in a tidal wave of our combined powers. Edan leaned against me against the wall breathing erratically as I was. Green, blue, and purple energy swirled around us and merged as his mark fully set in. Slowly, they separated again, but a small connection remained between us. After releasing my neck, he rested his forehead against mine.

"You okay?"

"Yeah," I wheezed.

"Your power is almost endless," he whispered.

His was endless. Somehow, he could tap into the other dragons and use theirs. Could I do that to the demons?

"Tora?"

"Hm?" I asked and looked up at him.

"You okay?"

I nodded and then bit his neck, drawing blood before releasing him.

"What was that?" he asked.

"Nothing, I just wanted to bite you too," I said and skipped down the hallway towards his mother who had stepped out of the room ahead of us with her hands on her hips.

Edan chuckled behind me and then jogged to catch up to me.

CHAPTER FOUR

My fingers twitched nervously as I opened a portal to the demon realm. One thing I had learned early on was not to disobey Father. So, Edan and I stood beside each other three days after our battle to visit him as he had ordered us.

"It's going to be fine," Edan assured me, his hand in mine.

"I can never tell with him," I muttered. He was temperamental to say the least.

"He already said he approved of our match," he reminded me.

Today he had opted for a pair of slacks and a dress shirt. He looked ready to conduct a business meeting and yet still incredibly scrumptious.

"You're ogling me again," he said with a smirk.

"Was not," I lied and focused on the portal before us, being sure to open it into the castle, specifically the throne room.

"We could be a few more minutes late," he offered in a husky voice.

"You're terrible," I accused before stepping through and pulling Edan into the demon world with me.

The room was empty save for Father on his throne. He was glaring at the wall while strumming his fingers on his throne. I hurried forward and bowed before him.

"Ah, you are here," he said in greeting.

"As you requested," I agreed.

"Stand."

I obeyed and stood beside Edan as we faced my father. "Why did you ask us here?"

"You are Princess and in order to court you, Edan has to pass a few tests," Father explained with a smirk.

I groaned. "Really? You're going to make him go through the tests?"

"Yes."

"He won't be able to break the records," I said smugly.

"I'm standing right here," Edan reminded me.

"Sorry, but you won't break the records."

"And if I do?" Edan asked.

"If you break the records, I will marry you on the spot," Father said.

"What!" I screamed.

"Quiet. I could have married you off to some random demon eons ago."

"You already gave us your approval," I reminded him.

"Yes, but he still has to pass the tests."

"And if he doesn't?"

"Then you won't be allowed to wed."

"This is ludicrous," I growled.

"Don't make me put you in the dungeon," Father threatened.

It wasn't an idle threat.

"What type of tests?" Edan asked Father.

"If I told you beforehand, that would ruin the fun," Father replied with a smile.

"You don't have to do this," I reminded Edan softly.

He looked at me with fire in his eyes and sternly said, "I will do this, so that I can marry you."

"Okay, but you still won't beat the records."

Edan bent down and kissed me. "Don't faint after witnessing my glory."

I rolled my eyes. "I'll try to contain myself."

Dad walked up to me and twirled his finger as though wrapping a string around it and tugged. It felt as though he jerked on my heart. "What is this?"

"Ow!" I snapped. "Stop."

"Did you mark her?" he asked Edan.

Edan nodded his head.

"But you haven't marked him yet?" Dad asked.

"Wait, you can mark me too?" Edan asked.

"Demon marks are different," I mumbled. "They have different side effects."

"Why didn't you tell me?" Edan asked.

"I had to talk to Dad first about the side effects. I've never done it before, so I wanted to check with him about something that I've heard."

"We'll talk later," Dad promised.

He snapped his fingers and transported us to the Pits, a large area they'd filled with sand to make an arena and surrounded with stands that were filled with demons, ready to watch.

"You already summoned everyone?" I asked.

Dad smiled. "Duh."

Edan stood in the center of the pit facing Tarlok, the strongest demon, next to my father. Tarlok looked up at me and blew me a kiss. "I'll make this quick so I can spend some time with you, Princess."

"What's the test?" Edan asked.

"You have to defeat Tarlok, our strongest fighter," Dad explained.

"Why am I not fighting the one who has the record?" he asked.

"The record is how fast you can defeat Tarlok," I explained.

"What's the record?"

"Two and a half minutes," Dad answered.

"No problem," Edan said with a cocky smirk.

"Princess, when I finish this you'll owe me a kiss."

"You only get a kiss if you defeat me."

"Then I'll defeat the dragon and you next."

"You won't be defeating me or getting a kiss from her," Edan growled.

Tarlok winked at me and Edan growled loudly. His skin shifted, but instead of taking on his dragon form, he shifted his skin into scales that glimmered like polished steel.

"I didn't know he could do that," I whispered in shock.

Tarlok smiled and then shifted into a larger version of his demon form. "This is going to be fun."

"You've pissed me off, so I won't be going easy on you," Edan informed him.

"Kick his ass!" I yelled.

Tarlok bowed to me and said, "As the Princess wishes."

"She was talking to me!" Edan growled and lashed out at Tarlok with clawed hands.

The two began moving so fast, that I could hardly keep track of them.

"He's quite talented," Dad said as he watched Edan closely.

"Why are you really doing this?" I asked without taking my eyes off of the fight.

"He appears strong, but I have to make sure that he'll be strong enough to protect you," he replied.

"That's dumb. I'm not going to stop seeing him if he doesn't meet your strength requirements."

"It's not about that, child. If he isn't strong enough, then I'll have to either make you stronger or make him stronger."

Oh.

"You can do that?"

He smiled and it sent chills down my spine. "There's a lot of things I can do that you don't know about."

"About the marking..."

"Unlike Dragons, it's permanent for us," he informed her.

"That's what I thought."

"I would suggest waiting until after you're mated. Not that you listen to me anyway..."

I rolled my eyes and then stared in shock at Edan standing over Tarlok, unconscious on the ground. "What?"

"How long?" Dad asked one of the demons beside him.

"Two minutes flat."

"Shit," I grumbled. He had beaten my time.

"Impressive," Dad said and clapped his hands.

The crowd cheered while Edan flexed and posed for them.

"Oh brother," I mumbled.

A couple demons drug Tarlok out of the arena to get ready for the next test.

I flew down with a bottle of water and held it out to him.

"Cooling yourself off after witnessing me?" he asked.

I rolled my eyes and handed it to him. "Yes," I lied.

"What's the next test?" he asked as he chugged some water.

"I didn't know you could grow scales in human form," I said instead of answering him.

"There's a lot of things I can do that you don't know about yet," he purred and kissed my cheek.

"Ten minute break," Dad called down.

"No tips or hints?" Edan asked.

"No, you already beat the first test's record," I snapped.

"Oh, come on, what's the next one?"

"You'll have to wait to find out," I said despite the nervousness that I felt. The next test was one I was not looking forward to.

I gave him a deep kiss and then Dad clapped his hands and I disappeared from the arena. I opened my eyes and groaned. I was chained inside of a cage, which hung over lava inside of a dungeon. Edan would have to find me and rescue me before time ran out. If he failed, the cage would fall into the lava and I would die.

"Why me?" I asked angrily.

"You're the only thing he'll care about saving," Dad answered. He provided me a view of Edan so I could watch his progress. Edan had shifted and was roaring angrily. "He's rather upset."

"Explain it quickly. I'd rather not be dropped into lava."

"Where is she!" Edan bellowed.

"That's for you to figure out. You have thirty minutes to

rescue her before she's dropped into lava and burned alive."

"She's your daughter!" He yelled.

"Son, I'm the Demon King. I can make more heirs."

Dad was rather convincing. It made my blood run cold. Well, if it could.

Edan roared again and then closed his eyes and stood very still. I felt a tug on our connection. He tugged once more and then opened his eyes.

"Found her," he replied smugly.

"Knowing her location and rescuing her are two different things," Dad replied and returned the smugness tenfold.

Edan growled and headed out of the arena.

"I'll provide some screens for you to watch his progress," Dad informed me.

"Thanks," I muttered.

Three screens appeared in front of me, offering several views of Edan as he marched down the hallways towards the dungeon. He pushed open the first door and Kerberos growled and barked at him with all three heads at the same time.

Edan smirked and then roared at Kerberos, his roar shook everything even down to where I was, the cage rattled. Kerberos, not one to be deterred by a good roar, rushed forward, each head coming in at a different angle to bite him. Edan's body shifted, becoming taller and broader, his face grew a snout and his hands turned into dragon talons. He dodged the heads and leapt up on top of Kerberos' back.

"Don't kill him!" I screamed and gripped my cage's bars.

Edan paused with his talon just above Kerberos' jugular.

"You may proceed," Dad informed him. "Kerberos, down."

Kerberos lay down and huffed angrily.

Edan shifted back into his human form and continued past Kerberos into the next hallway. I didn't think he could actually hear me. Had he heard me? Or had Dad stopped him?

The next hallway was pitch black, but Edan's eyes began to glow and somehow, I knew that it allowed him to see. That was a skill that would definitely come in handy.

Something cold and wet dripped from the ceiling onto Edan's face. He wiped it with the back of his hand and looked up just as several small goblin shaped clay creatures fell onto him. He grabbed them and tossed them away, but there were dozens and they kept coming. He threw a bunch in front of him and then exhaled a jet of flames over them. They hardened, broke, and then turned to dust. Dozens more came and no matter how many times he repeated the process, more came to replace their fallen brethren.

Edan growled angrily, but continued doing what he was doing.

Tarlok appeared next to me and smiled. "Sorry about this," he whispered.

"About what?" I asked.

He stabbed my leg and twisted the knife. I screamed in pain and tried to grab it from him.

Edan's head jerked up and his entire body glowed. He roared and the hallway he was in filled with fire, destroying all of the clay goblins in an instant. He rushed forward, slamming the next doors open and nearly fell face first into a pit of spikes.

Tarlok removed the knife and then healed my leg.

"I'm going to get you back for that," I promised him.

"King's orders," he explained and then disappeared.

I grumbled angrily, but there was little I could do about it.

Edan grew wings and flew over the pit of spikes to land on a small square of land. All around it were spikes and directly above him were three harpies.

The harpies swooped down onto him, but he took flight and began to fight them in a deadly aerial combat.

"Will you be stabbing me again?" I asked.

"No, that was the last time," Dad said and I knew he was smiling.

"You could have just asked me to yell."

"I had to make it convincing. Plus, he can feel whether you're in pain through your connection."

"What? How?"

"It's a Dragon thing," he replied vaguely. "Their connections work differently than others."

"Good to know."

Edan defeated the harpies, their bodies strewn about over spikes, and continued on. The next room was my favorite room. The minotaur.

The minotaur snorted at Edan as he entered and pawed the ground.

"A minotaur? You own a minotaur?"

"He attacked Tora when she was a child and this is his punishment," Dad explained.

That minotaur was the first I had ever seen and had almost killed me.

"So, if I kill him, I won't be in trouble?" Edan asked.

"Bring it on, little boy," the minotaur threatened Edan.

"Time is running out," Dad reminded him.

Edan fully shifted into his dragon form and charged the minotaur. The minotaur dropped his head down and charged Edan. Edan blasted the minotaur with fire and then latched onto him with his thick jaws. The minotaur bellowed in pain and tried to break free, but Edan didn't let go.

"This is a little one sided," I whispered.

"He has two more steps," Dad reminded me.

Edan pushed through the next hallway still in is dragon form. You could see his rage seething off of him like steam. Why was he so mad? He had agreed to do this. I should be the mad one. I was the one locked in a cage that hung over lava.

I was still two floors below him. Dad changed the opponents constantly, so I had no idea what he would face next. What I did not expect was for him to crash straight through the floor to get to me. He landed on top of my cage, making the cage sway around.

"Ah!" I screamed.

"Hello beautiful," he said after shifting to his human form.

"Having fun?" I asked.

"What caused you pain earlier?" he asked and broke the lock on my cage.

"Being stabbed in the leg," I explained and showed him the blood dried on my leg.

He growled and tore the door off of the cage. "This was not what I thought would happen."

"You're not even to the final event yet," I informed him.

He wrapped his arm around my waist and leapt back up through the hole he had created. "What's the final event?"

Dad clapped his hands and Edan and I stood in the center of the arena. "The final event," Dad said with a smile. "Is to defeat the previous record holder in a match to death, knockout, or submission."

I brushed myself off and stretched my sore muscles.

"Who is the previous record holder?" Edan asked, pumped to start fighting.

I swung my leg around and knocked his legs out from under him with a wide smile on my face. "Me."

He chuckled and stood back up. "I should have known."

Taking a defensive stance, I raised my hands up and whispered, "Bring it on, Prince."

"Which form would you prefer?" he asked me as he circled me slowly.

The response I almost blurted was not one to be said with my Dad watching. "Whichever you think will be able to defeat me," I replied instead.

He smirked and then shifted into his dragon form.

My smile widened and I let out more of my demonic power, letting my body shift into my true form, the one I could take only when in the Demon Realm. While in the Demon Realm, I could grow to stand ten feet tall and my body grew within proportion. I flexed my wings out and roared at him.

Edan roared back and charged me. I jumped up over his head and landed on his back, Before I could wrap my hands around his neck, he rolled onto his back and pinned me beneath him.

"Lazy," I grunted and bit into his shoulder.

He growled in pain and rolled away to let me up.

I wanted to fight him, but I didn't want to kill him. It

presented a lot of issues for me considering my normal fighting style was to kill. He shifted forms again, going back to his human form, and leapt up onto my back with his arm around my throat.

I cut one of his arms with my tail, grabbed with one hand and tossed him up and over me.

"I could end this by roasting you, but I'd rather keep your hair on your head," he told me.

"I'm trying to figure out how *not* to kill you," I admitted.

He chuckled and I felt his power open a moment before he disappeared. I turned around, trying to find him, but saw the puff of dirt from his last location too late. He pinned me to the ground with his teeth around my throat.

"Edan wins!" Dad announced.

"Cheater," I grumbled.

He kissed my neck and whispered, "Once you know all of my tricks, our sparring matches will be much harder. I had to take you down quickly while I still could."

I let him pull me up and shrank back to my normal height.

"I have to say, having a girlfriend that much taller than me is very strange."

I chuckled and kissed his lips. "Lucky for you, I only get that tall here in the Demon Realm."

"As the winner, I give you my full consent and blessing for your relationship."

"Thanks," I mumbled while Edan smiled proudly.

"And, with that, Edan and I must speak alone."

"Why?" I asked nervously.

"Man business," Dad said with a wink. He set his hand on Edan's shoulder and the two disappeared.

"Wonderful," I growled.

I transported myself to my room in the castle and flopped down onto my bed with a sigh. I'd lost. I couldn't believe that I'd lost a fight. Edan had defeated me in front of my dad and my entire race. Would my dad make me do extra training since I had embarrassed the demon race?

CHAPTER FIVE

Edan refused to tell me what my dad had discussed with him, so I spent the next day sulking on my couch while Emily baked me cookies.

"I know it's frustrating to lose," she said as she mixed the dough. "But isn't it a good thing to find a boyfriend who is stronger than you?"

"I'm not upset about losing."

She tilted her head as she looked at me.

"Okay, I am upset about that, but that's not why I'm sulking. My dad and he spent two hours talking and he refuses to tell me what they discussed."

"He passed the tests, so he approves of your relationship, which means it can't be anything bad."

"It's my dad," I reminded her. "It could always be bad."

"I'm sure it's nothing," she said and tried to console me.

She brought me out a small bowl of cookie dough with a spoon.

"I love you," I whispered and took a big bite.

Someone knocked on the door and Emily went to answer it. She opened the door and sputtered nonsense before backing away.

Dad walked inside and I stared in disbelief at him.

"Hello is the appropriate greeting here," he told me.

"What? Why? What are you doing here?" I asked angrily.

"No one saw me come in," he promised.

"Why are you here?" I asked.

"I need to talk to you," he explained.

"Emily, this is my dad," I said and waved at her.

She came over and curtsied to him. "Your Highness."

He smiled and bowed. "It is an honor to meet you, Emily. You've been a wonderful friend for my daughter."

"Thank you," she whispered.

"Em, can you give us a moment?" I asked.

She nodded and left the dorm room immediately.

"What's going on?" I asked nervously. He'd never visited me at the college before.

"There was something I didn't tell you," he began. "When Demon royalty begins a serious relationship, they create a contract with their significant other."

"A contract?"

"In order to ensure that we aren't taken advantage of or harmed, we make a contract with them to ensure everything goes well."

"Are you saying that I have to make a contract with Edan?" I asked as fear constricted my throat.

He nodded. "I already told him about it. He's aware of the type of contract you would need to create and what would happen should he break it."

Oh no. That was why he wouldn't talk to me about it.

"I guess that means our relationship is over," I whispered sadly. "And I finally found someone who didn't care I was a demon. I didn't think it would end like this."

"Not so fast," Edan said.

I growled, startled that he had appeared without me hearing.

"You scared me," I whispered.

"You're so quick to give up on us."

"I'm not giving up on us!" I snapped. "I don't want us to end."

"Then let's hash out the contract."

"Edan, are you sure? A contract with a demon…"

"It's not a contact with a random demon. It's a contract with you, my girlfriend."

"This isn't a decision to be taken lightly."

"Why are you so scared?" Edan asked softly.

"This one doesn't seem inclined to kill you," Dad noted.

I growled. "Thanks for pointing that out."

Dad sighed. "Daughter, I understand that you're dealing with something unknown to you. This is something that is done to protect you and I won't allow you to continue without doing this. The contract can be cancelled by you at any time. It won't harm him unless he does something against the terms and conditions. And, you get to write those."

"Are you sure?" I asked Edan.

He smiled and said, "I've never been more sure of something in my life."

"Alright," I mumbled.

"Let's get this contract worked out."

Dad set down a thick document on the coffee table and then sat in the corner of the couch. "I'll be here if you have questions."

"You already had one written?" I asked in disbelief.

"You're my only daughter and my heir. I had this written when you were five."

I wasn't certain if I should be offended or pleased.

Edan snapped his fingers and his assistant appeared next to him. "You rang, sir?"

Edan pointed at the stack. "Brief this please."

He bowed to me. "A pleasure to see you again, Princess."

I inclined my head. "It's nice to see you as well."

He looked over at Dad in shock and then bowed to him. "Your Highness."

Dad smirked and inclined his head. "Nice to meet you."

Pleasantries out of the way, he put on a pair of glasses, chanted a spell, and then went through the entire document in two minutes.

He removed the glasses and tucked them in his shirt pocket. "You cheat on her, try to harm her, harm her, or anything a typical boyfriend shouldn't do and she gets your soul for ten years."

"*Dad*," I groaned.

"It's hardly a punishment," Dad argued.

"And if she does any of those things?" Edan asked.

"You are allowed to punish her as you see fit, aside from permanent mutilation or death," his assistant answered.

"That's a rather broad area for interpretation," I commented.

Dad shrugged. "I figured you would be smart enough not to do anything to warrant punishment."

"The contract expires once you are married or once one of you dies," the assistant explained further.

"Anything you think needs changing?" Edan asked.

He had a lot of faith in his assistant. It made me view him in a different light.

"No. It's a pretty basic contract as far as royal courting goes."

Dad looked at me smugly.

Yeah, eat it up. I wasn't going to give you the satisfaction of saying anything.

"Great, thank you," Edan said and dismissed him.

Dad held out a pen and a knife to Edan. "Whenever you're ready."

"What happens after I sign and apply a blood fingerprint?" Edan asked.

"Then Tora seals the contract with you and you're both marked."

"The mark is permanent," I explained to Edan. "Even if we break the contract and go our separate ways, I will always have the mark with you and be able to locate you."

"I'm aware."

I wanted to ask if he was sure again, but bit my tongue. "It's been a long time since I've done one," I reminded Dad.

"You'll be fine," he said with no encouragement

whatsoever.

"You've done one before?" Edan asked.

"Not for this, but I've made a contract before," I explained.

"For what?" Edan asked.

I held out my arm to show him my talisman, currently a bracelet. "To have this made. It has my blood in it, so I wanted to make sure that he didn't do anything else with my blood or do anything funny to the talisman."

He relaxed a bit and then signed his name on the contract. I felt a tug in my core as he signed, the document already tied to me by Dad's magic. Edan cut his thumb and then pressed a bloody thumbprint to the document. I took the pen from him, signed, put my thumbprint and then rested my hand against the center of his chest.

"Contract number two has been signed by both parties. This contract will remain in effect until marriage, death of one or both of the signees, or by my will. Do you agree, Prince Edan of the Dragons?"

"I agree."

My magic gathered, my body changed, and I drove a red tether into Edan's soul. He growled, but didn't move.

"Our contract is sealed."

"Our contract is sealed," Edan repeated.

"You are marked and though the contract may end, the mark will never disappear."

"Understood."

"What was that?" Edan's mother asked with a snarl as she threw open my door.

Dad was up and standing between us before I could even react. She looked at him and her eyes widened.

"Easy," I whispered.

Dad teleported back to the couch and looked as though he had never moved.

"Just tying the final knots for our courting," Edan explained.

She exhaled and ran a hand through her hair. "You should have warned me. I freaked out."

"Sorry," he apologized.

"You marked him, right?" she asked.

I nodded.

"Well, now it's official. Now you're under a Demonic Contract," she said with a wide smile. I'd never met someone who had smiled about their son being bound to a contract with a demon before.

"Picture!" she ordered. Dad was one step ahead of her and set up a camera on the far side of the room.

Edan kissed the side of my head and whispered, "Tomorrow we are running away from them for a few days."

I nodded and then leaned my head against his chest, hearing his heartbeat and feeling him through our dual markings.

We stood together and his mother said, "Everyone say, 'Demonic Contract.'"

"Demonic Contract!" we said as the camera took the picture.

ABOUT THE AUTHOR

Catherine Banks is a bestselling fantasy author who writes in several fantasy subgenres under two pseudonyms. She began writing fiction at only four years old and finished her first full-length novel at the age of fifteen. She is married to her soulmate and best friend, Avery, who she has two amazing children with. After her full time job, she reads books, plays video games, and watches anime shows and movies with her family to relax. Although she has lived in Northern California her entire life, she dreams of traveling around the world. Catherine is also C.E.O. of Turbo Kitten Industries™, a company with many hats including being a book publisher and Etsy store full of nerdy fun.